To Shiloh on her first birthday.
Love,
Stanley and Rena

Before I formed you in the womb I knew you.
Jeremiah 1:5

THIS LITTLE LIGHT OF MINE

by Claire Boudreaux Bateman

Illustrations by Katie Norwood Alexander

Published in the United States 2005 by Shell Beach Publishing
6010 Perkins Road, Suite A, Baton Rouge, LA 70808

Art Direction by Chris Steiner

Digital Photography by David Humphreys

ISBN 978-0-9706732-2-0

ISBN 0-9706732-2-1

Printed in China

Second Edition

www.howchristmasbegan.com

SPECIAL THANKS

Rev. Chris Andrews, Renee Bacher, Kay Blake, Fr. Donald Blanchard, Lisette Borné, Fr. Gerald Burns,

Rachel and Michael DiResto, Rachel Hadley, Julie Hoffman, Alyce-Elise Hoge, Paige and James Fontenot, Kelli Scott Kelley,

Elena and Kyle Keegan, Sonia Levitin, Lucy Smith, Kristen Reed, Debbie Vollmer and Dr. B.J. Zamora

To God's undeniable light in David, Drew and Avery Claire

cbb

To my sweet boys Christopher, John Christopher and Barrow,
Your radiant light makes the world a brighter place. This is for you.

kna

WE all come from a
very special place in heaven.

Here, angels sweetly tell us about life on earth.
"These are your ears," said one angel. "With
them you will hear the beautiful sounds of the
world, like birds and water and singing."

"These are your eyes," said another angel. "With these you will see all of the gifts God has made on earth. And look down here, you have two feet and ten toes, my little one. You won't believe how much you will use these on earth."

"Okay, let's see," the last angel said.

"Eyes, eyelashes? Check.

Eyebrows, elbows, fingers, toes? Yes. Yes. Yes. Yes.

Okay. Good, little one, everything looks fine."

The angel turned
to all of heaven and
announced, "It's a girl,
and we are ready to
turn on her light!"

The little one found herse

waiting in a **long, long** line.

When she made it to the front of the line
she saw God. "Come to me, little one,"
God said. "Let me have a look at you."

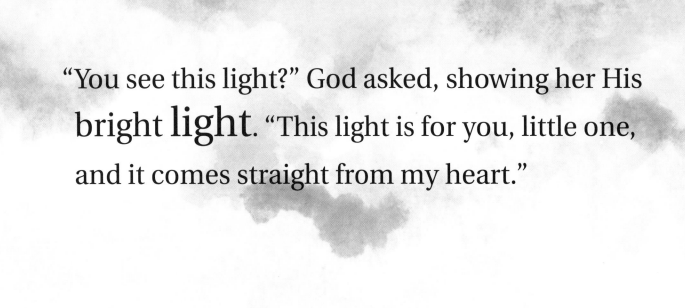

"You see this light?" God asked, showing her His bright **light**. "This light is for you, little one, and it comes straight from my heart."

She knew the light was special and worried out loud, "What if I lose the light, God?"

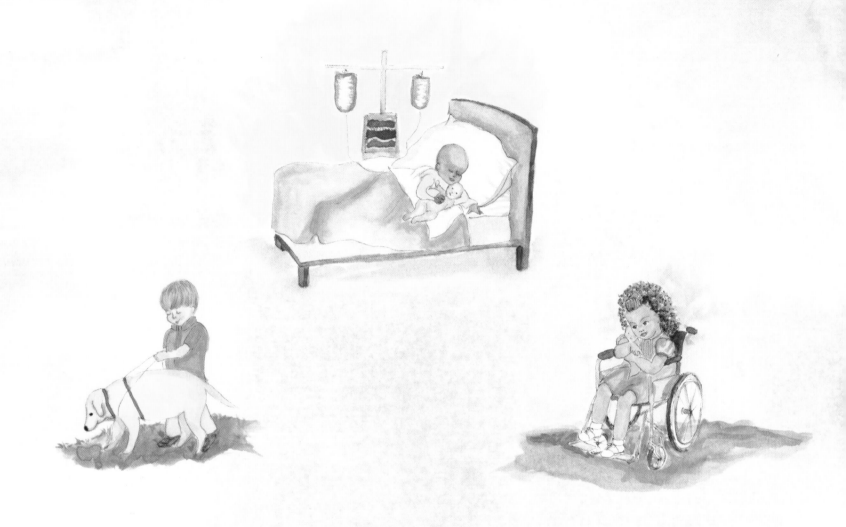

"It's impossible to lose this light," God said. "On your way to earth, you may lose your eyes or your ears. While you are on earth, you may get sick and lose all of your hair. But my light will always be in you."

"What do I do with the light, God?" she asked.

"This light is made of my love, little one. You will use it to love others, and your kindness will lead you right back to me. You will recognize the light in people when they are sweet or forgiving."

"You see, little one, I have given my light to everyone."

"Everyone?" she asked. "What about people who are different from me?"

"They have all been on my lap," God answered.

The little one thought about everything God had said. She liked it here with Him.

"God?"

"Yes, little light of mine?"

"How will I remember you?"

God was happy to answer her question.

He knew this soul was almost ready to go.

"Once a year you will celebrate your trip to earth.
As part of the celebration you will see a light,"
He said. "This will remind you of me.
As you grow and love all the people of the world,
you will notice the light gets brighter and brighter,"
God explained.

Seeing the cake, God's light, and the happy faces on earth made her so excited she began to float.
"I am on my way, God. My light will shine for all the world to see!"

"I know it will,"

God said, as His little light

safely made her way to earth.

"I know it will."